The Adventures of Arrow

A Selection Of Short Stories

by Buck Kalinowski

Illustrations by Kimberly Miller

Printed in Victoria, Canada

National Library of Canada Cataloguing in Publication

Kalinowski, Buck, 1958-
 The adventures of Arrow / Buck Kalinowski ;
illustrated by Kimberly Miller.
ISBN 1-55369-595-X
 I. Miller, Kim II. Title.
PZ7.K14154Ad 2002   j813'.6   C2002-902471-4

TRAFFORD

This book was published *on-demand* in cooperation with Trafford Publishing.
On-demand publishing is a unique process and service of making a book available for retail sale to the public taking advantage of on-demand manufacturing and Internet marketing. **On-demand publishing** includes promotions, retail sales, manufacturing, order fulfilment, accounting and collecting royalties on behalf of the author.

Suite 6E, 2333 Government St., Victoria, B.C. V8T 4P4, CANADA
Phone   250-383-6864   Toll-free   1-888-232-4444 (Canada & US)
Fax   250-383-6804   E-mail   sales@trafford.com
Web site   www.trafford.com   TRAFFORD PUBLISHING IS A DIVISION OF TRAFFORD HOLDINGS LTD.
Trafford Catalogue #02-0408   www.trafford.com/robots/02-0408.html

10   9   8   7   6   5   4   3   2

Acknowledgments

Special thanks to Patricia Hamilton for her editing "The Adventures of Arrow", and to Sarah Kalinowski, a teacher, for reading to her class and their editorial comments.

To Bryan Page for the cover photo retouching, Barbara Lazarski for her cover design and layout of the book, and to Bo Page for her constant support of all Farmer Buck's endeavors.

Thanks to all the people at Hillside that help to take care of Cupid & Arrow, staff, their blacksmith Kyle Gavin, and The Hillside Equestrian Shoppe that keeps them outfitted and groomed to perfection.

To all the children who continue to shower their love and affection to Cupid, a true miracle horse, and her son Arrow.

Introduction

This is the story of a little horse named Arrow.

You see, Arrow was born around Valentine's Day, and from the very beginning, he received lots of attention. He was little and cute and had a special mark. Centered across his rump was a big white patch of fur shaped like an arrow pointing to his head. It really stuck out on his little brown body. Arrow's mother was pretty special too. She had a perfect heart-shaped mark on her forehead, and her name was Cupid.

Cupid had had a hard life and things did not come easy for her. She had met many people who were not very nice while she was growing up. Then one day a kind farmer bought her at an auction and changed her life forever. Cupid was now a sweet and gentle horse who knew how to behave. She had known many horses and had heard lots of stories about people who had little patience and would not take the time to teach horses the proper way. Cupid knew that to be loved you must show love and be able to forgive. Sometimes, you had to try again when things didn't go right and never give up.

Once Arrow was born, Cupid had her job cut out for her with her little son. Everyone wanted to see the new colt; after all, how many horses in the world have an arrow on their rump? There are brown horses and black horses, golden horses and spotted horses; some have stars on their faces while others have stripes of white, but only one horse has an arrow.

Arrow liked meeting people. He enjoyed being petted and liked running around when the farm workers would let him out for exercise. Arrow was always getting into something, and that is why this book is called **The Adventures of Arrow.**

_____

Dedication

This book is dedicated to Alexie Page who was born blind and had a deep fear of horses. Today she has overcome those fears and has fallen in love with a horse in this book. My prayer for her is that she will someday see the horse that she has come to love and ride.

The Adventures of Arrow

A Selection Of Short Stories

A Summer Lesson

One spring morning, Arrow and Cupid were out in Farmer Buck's big backyard. It had a long wooden fence and two big willow trees that were a favorite place to stay cool on hot sunny days. The grass was tall and fresh water waited in a big tub when the horses got thirsty. Flowers bloomed around the wishing well that stood in the field. Farmer Buck would pick certain horses every day to roam in this special yard, and today it was Cupid's and Arrow's turn.

"Bark! Bark! Bark!" came a sound from the back porch of Farmer Buck's house as a little dog ran down the stairs.

"Hey, there! You're new," said Jack, Farmer Buck's little dog.

Arrow thought Jack was cute and very interesting. This was the first time he had seen a dog.

"Do you want to play?" asked Jack.

Arrow checked with his mom, who said "yes". She told him to play nice and not to go too far. Jack began to run and Arrow followed him. The dog ran around the big willow tree and so did Arrow. Jack jumped over the flowers and Arrow was close behind. "This is fun!" Arrow shouted as they ran across the field.

Then the little dog ran under the fence and cried, "You can't catch me!"

CRASH! Arrow hit the fence boards and fell down right on his famous bottom. "Are you okay?" Jack asked.

A bit dazed, Arrow sat there until Cupid trotted over and gently licked her son's head.

"You have to watch where you're going my little one."

"Ouch!" Arrow thought. "Playing can be rough, but it was fun to meet a new friend today."

"See ya tomorrow, Arrow," Jack barked. "Maybe we'll play again."

The next day Arrow lay in the field warming his body in the sun. Cupid was eating the lush green grass nearby.

"Bark! Bark! Bark! "Hi, Arrow! Let's play!"
"I'm tired from yesterday," Arrow replied.

"Come on!" barked Jack. "Get up and follow me!"

Cupid came over and asked Jack to stop barking.

"Will you chase me today?" Jack asked.

Cupid said, "Not today. I am going to eat and watch my son."

"Bark! Bark! Bark! I want to play!" said Jack. Jack tried to nip at Cupid's legs so she would chase him.

"Stop it," said Cupid.

Then Jack pulled on Cupid's tail.

"Ouch!" Cupid screeched, and with that she picked up her foot and gave the dog a swift kick.

"Yipe! Yipe! Yipe!" Jack squealed and headed back to the house with his head hung low and his tail between his legs.

Farmer Buck saw the whole thing from his back porch. "That's what you get, Jack," he said, rubbing his dog's head. "Thanks for going easy on him!" he yelled to Cupid.   "You have to learn to take "No" for an answer sometimes. There are going to be days when you want to be left alone, too. You keep pestering, you might get another one of those kicks."

Jack seemed to understand and went to lie down in his doggie bed.

"You'll feel better after your nap," said Farmer Buck. "Pleasant dreams." And the tired little dog went to sleep.

A Summer Lesson

1. Instead of biting, what should Jack have done when Cupid said she didn't want to play?

2. What could Cupid have done rather than kicking Jack after he bit her?

Stay Away From The Water

As Arrow was growing, word began to spread in the little town of Wolcott, Connecticut, that a horse with a heart marking gave birth to a baby with an arrow. People came from all over to see this miracle colt. One morning Cupid heard Farmer Buck say that she and Arrow would be having their exercise in the little pasture down by the pond. Cupid thought, 'Oh good! This will keep that little dog Jack from bothering Arrow today.'

Cupid and Arrow lived at a farm named Hillside. It was a big place with over a hundred horses. After their morning breakfast of grain, the horses were led out of their stalls by the farm workers.

Cupid and Arrow were taken to a quiet little pasture by the water. It was a beautiful spring day, and a light breeze blew across the pond as Crackle and Pop, the farm's ducks, were drifting along the water's edge. As the horses were let out, Arrow spotted Crackle and asked, "What are you? You don't look like a dog, and you have a big nose."

"I'm a duck," said Crackle. "Would you like to play with us?"

Arrow asked his mom if it would be all right and she said yes. "But remember to be careful. You know what happened when you played with Jack," she warned.

Crackle and Pop walked around on the grass, and Arrow followed behind. He thought they walked funny. As the ducks ran faster, Arrow tried to step on Crackle's tail. He remembered Jack doing something like that.

The outraged duck let out a loud "Quack! Quack! Quack!" and flew off the dock and into the water.

"Wow! How did you do that?" Arrow asked.

Crackle wanted to have some fun with Arrow and decided to play a little joke on him.   "It's easy. All you do is jump into the air and float in the water like this," said the duck. Then Pop jumped off the dock and softly landed on the cool pond water.

"Gee! That looks cool. Here I come!" said Arrow.

Cupid saw her little colt running toward the pond. "No! No!" yelled the horse.
"You're not a duck." But it was too late. Off the dock he jumped, up into the
air and SPLASH! At first, it was hard to see anything, but then up popped his
little head, and those spindly legs began to kick in the water. Arrow wasn't
swimming exactly, and he wasn't floating very well either.

"Get out of that water!" Cupid yelled.

The young horse made his way back to land and climbed out of the muddy water. His legs and body were covered with black mud, and his white Arrow was no longer there.

'Where did it go?' Cupid wondered. The mud had covered it, and Arrow now looked like one of the black little ponies in the pasture next door. By mid-day, the farm workers noticed that a black pony was with Cupid, but where was Arrow?

"Arrow is missing!" "Call Farmer Buck!" "Call the police!" "Someone has stolen Arrow!" The police arrived and asked if anyone saw the colt leave the farm.

Arrow wondered what everyone was talking about. "I'm right here," he thought. Cupid was led back to her stall, and the little black Arrow was put with the little black ponies. "Wait a minute. I'm Arrow!"

"Sure you are," said Jack, who was sitting on the hilltop watching for the missing horse.

"Really, I am! Remember when we played the other day, and I hit my head on the fence?"

"Well, if you're Arrow, where is your marking?"
Arrow said, "I was in the pond and now it's covered with mud."

Jack knew that Arrow was telling the truth, but how would he be able to tell Farmer Buck? "I have a plan. If I open your pen tonight, follow me to the house." Nighttime fell and Farmer Buck let Jack out to go to the bathroom. Jack stopped on the porch as farmer Buck looked up in the star lit sky and prayed, "Dear Lord, you know where little Arrow is, please keep him safe and bring him home again to this farm and his friends cause we all miss him very much, Amen.' Just then Jack looked at his water dish, and began to pant.

"Well, drink up," said the farmer. " Your dish is half full."

Jack sniffed the water and panted some more.

"Okay, I'll get you some fresh water," Farmer Buck said as he carried Jack's dish into the house.

Jack knew he had to work fast, so off he ran as hard as he could to the pony corral. He even said a little prayer that his plan would work "Arrow, are you in there?" he barked.

"Here I am, Jack!" Arrow missed his mother and hoped that Jack's plan would work. Jumping up, the little dog opened the latch that held the gate closed and it slowly swung open.

"Follow me, Arrow!" Jack barked. Arrow walked out the gate and so did all the other ponies. "Let's go," Jack barked.

The ponies ran up the hill to the field behind Farmer Buck's house. Arrow stood under the porch as Jack told him to do. "Don't move. I'll be right back," Jack said.

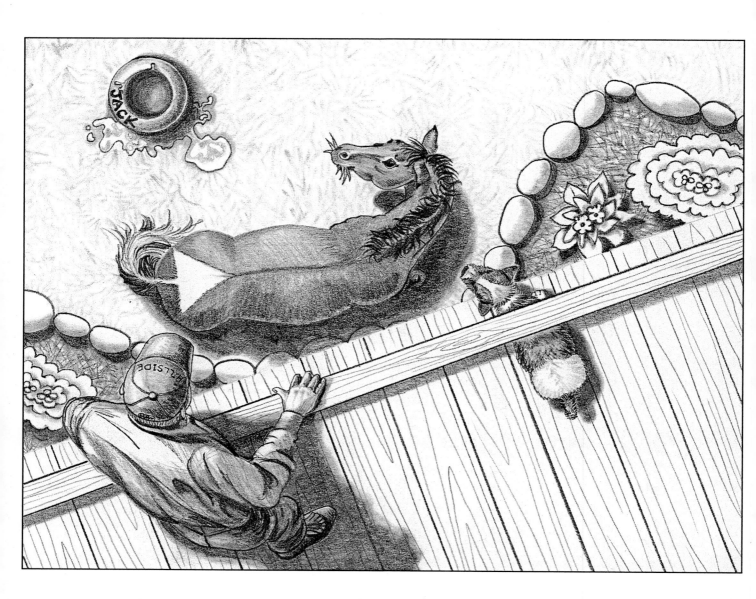

30

Farmer Buck came back with Jack's water dish just as his dog was climbing up the stairs. Although Jack was very thirsty from running around, he took his little nose and pushed the water dish over the edge of the porch and on top of Arrow's muddy back. Right on target! Farmer Buck looked at Jack and then looked at where the water dish had fallen. "There you are!" We have been looking for you all day."

Jack barked with joy at his pal.

"Thanks, Jack. I will help you someday, my friend," said the horse.

Jack began to bark to tell Farmer Buck that the ponies were out. 'How did that happen?' he wondered. It was Jack and Arrow's little secret. The happy colt was returned to his mother. He was very hungry for her warm milk.

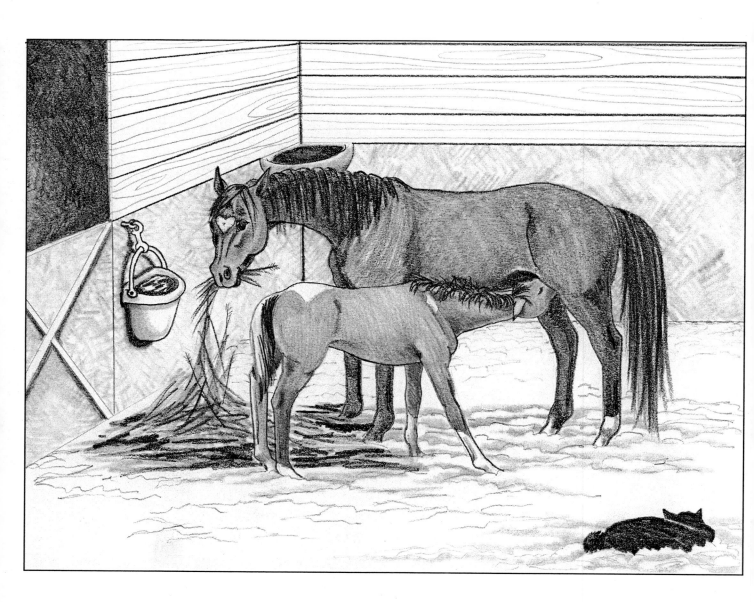

"I hope you learned your lesson today, Arrow " Cupid said ,as she nuzzled him. You are a horse, not a duck. But at least you're home safe. That night farmer Buck prayed and thanked God for bringing Arrow home safely. Jack curled up next to farmer Bucks pillow and even said a little prayer thanking God that his little pal was home safe again and tomorrow they could play again.

Stay away from the water

1. Why can't Arrow swim like the ducks can?
2. How was Jack being a friend to Arrow?
3. Should you always do what someone else does just because they asked you to?

Arrow Goes To Town

The next day Cupid and Arrow were taken to the big indoor arena. This was a large building where adults and children could ride indoors or horses could just run around while their stalls were cleaned by the farm workers. The horses loved to have clean stalls, just as parents want children's rooms to always be neat. Arrow liked the indoor. He often chased the cats as they crossed the arena. Sometimes the rooster jumped on his back, and Arrow would try to buck him off. The kids always wanted to give Cupid and Arrow treats, and the little colt had fun chasing them when the treats ran out.

Suddenly Arrow heard a noise and saw the farm truck with a big trailer coming down the hill. The engine on the truck was loud. As it got closer, the big metal trailer rattled as it drove down the gravel road. Cupid watched as the big gate to the indoor arena swung open. 'Is this a new horse?' he wondered.

Arrow had never seen anything like this before. The big truck and trailer came to a stop and out jumped Farmer Buck. "Hello, Cupid," he said. "I hope Arrow stays out of trouble today."

Cupid thought, 'Don't worry. He can't get lost in here.'

Miss Gail, the English trainer, opened the big door to the trailer and out came Checkers, a little black and white show pony. They must have been returning from a show.

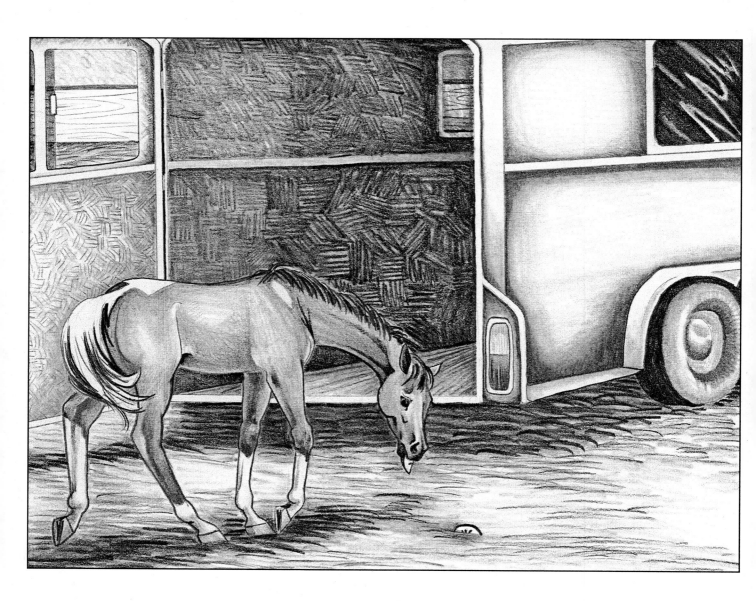

As the horses were led to their stalls, Arrow decided to take a closer look. Cupid was content eating some fresh hay, knowing her son couldn't go far inside the indoor arena. Arrow sniffed the tires of the big trailer and then slid his nose over the shiny fenders. As he approached the back of the trailer, he noticed someone had dropped a piece of apple on the ground. Arrow loved apples and decided to eat it. As he was slowly chewing his morning treat, he noticed that there was another one, only this piece was inside the trailer.

'I'm not going in there,' he thought. But then he remembered seeing three horses come out of there today. 'It's probably no big deal.' He looked over at his mother, who was still busy munching on her hay and decided not to bother her by asking for permission. Arrow stepped into the trailer and ate the other pieces of apple. He even found a little carrot! 'Wow,' he thought, 'these trailers have the best snacks!'

Just then Arrow heard Farmer Buck say, "I'm in a hurry. I have to go pick up a new pony." SLAM! The big trailer doors shut. Cupid watched as Farmer Buck got into his truck and drove out. Cupid whinnied, "Stand clear Arrow!" because she thought her colt was on the other side of the trailer. As the truck pulled out, Cupid saw Arrow in the trailer looking out the window. She ran to the gate, but it was too late. 'Now what has he gotten himself into?' she thought. 'Where is my little one going now?'

Arrow had never ridden in a trailer. It was bumpy, and he bounced around from side to side because he was not tied in a secure stall. 'Where is he taking me?' wondered the young colt.

42

As Farmer Buck drove up the hill, he waved to Emmy, who ran the tack store on the big farm. Arrow saw many new things. He saw the grocery store, the bank, a school with lots of children, a donut shop, and a gas station. At the intersection were lots of cars and trucks with big load motors. Arrow could still hear his mother's words over and over in his head: "Don't get into trouble" How will he get out of this mess? Where was he going? Will he ever see his friends back at the farm?

Farmer Buck drove his truck into the gas station. The gas attendant asked, "What would you like today, Farmer Buck?"

"Fill it up, please," he replied. As the gas man filled the truck, Farmer Buck heard a big commotion coming out of the trailer, so he decided to check it out. Bang! Bang! Bang! Farmer Buck opened the trailer door, and to his surprise, there was Arrow.

"What the heck are you doing in here?" he asked. "You have way too much time on your hands. Starting tomorrow we are going to use that energy to teach you some tricks.   Maybe then you will practice them when you have free time and develop a special talent when you get older." Farmer Buck paid the gas man and said, "Thanks."

As he was getting ready to drive the young horse back to the farm, he thought that this trip might be a good experience for Arrow. The horse would have to learn to travel correctly in the trailer someday, so it might as well be today. He first called the farm to tell the workers that he was taking Arrow with him to pick up the new pony. Farmer Buck did not want everyone worrying like they had the day before. The ride was about an hour away, and Arrow got to see lots of different things along the way. When they finally arrived, Arrow watched as they brought out a very fat and nervous pony.

"He is too much for my little girl to handle," said a big gruff man. "He is very hard to catch and keeps bucking her off. And he bites," said the man to Farmer Buck.

Arrow could see that these people didn't know too much about horses. There was rope tied to the pony's neck, and his barn was very messy with old windows containing broken glass. Kids were yelling and running around, making the little pony jump.

48

Farmer Buck knew that this pony needed some help.

They loaded the pony into the trailer and tied him next to Arrow. "What's your name?"

"My name is Arrow."

"My name is Griffen."

"Where are we going?" asked Griffen.

"I think we are going back home."

"Home," said the pony. "Where is that?"

"It's this place where I play with my friend Jack, and hang out with the ducks, and play with the children."

"What are you doing in here?" asked Griffen.
"Oh, I climbed in to eat a carrot. The next thing I knew the door shut, and

I couldn't get out."

"Did you get hit?" asked Griffen.

"No," replied Arrow.

"Did you get yelled at?"

"Nope."

"Get spanked?"

"No," replied Arrow. "I am only a baby."

Griffen told Arrow, "I want to be good, but when children hit me, I bite. Sometimes when they ride me, they hurt me with sticks, so I buck them off. I always run from them because they're so mean," said Griffen as a tear fell from his dirty face.

"Don't worry, Griffen. You'll like it here. Just give everyone who works with you a chance, and you'll be a happy pony again," Arrow said kindly. "Farmer Buck is going to start teaching me tricks. Then maybe I can teach you."

When they pulled into the farm, Cupid ran to the trailer and was thankful that her little colt was all right. "Here he is, Cupid!" said Farmer Buck. "Those quiet days on the farm just don't happen anymore with this little guy getting into everything. Tomorrow I am going to start teaching him some tricks. He needs to put that free time into something new to learn."

Arrow Goes To Town

1. Why should Arrow had asked his mom for permission before going into the trailer?

2. How could the children on Griffen's farm treated him with respect?

3. What was different from Arrows farm and Griffen's farm?

4. Why did farmer Buck call the farm?

52

Arrow Learns Some Tricks

The next afternoon Farmer Buck walked around the farm handing out carrots to all his special pals. As Arrow approached the fence, the farmer climbed over it with a carrot in his hand. "Well, Arrow," he said, "you are going to have to work for this one." He decided to teach his young horse a trick. Arrow was not sure what was going on, but he wanted that carrot.

"Today you are going to learn to bow."

'Bow? What is a bow?' Arrow wondered.

Farmer Buck placed the carrot in front of Arrow's nose. As Arrow went to bite it, the farmer moved the carrot down toward Arrow's chest. Arrow stretched his little neck and ate it. "Good boy, Arrow!" he said as he pet the colt on the neck. "Now let's see you go even lower." This time Farmer Buck went lower with the carrot. Down, down, down he went until the carrot was under the horse's belly, and lower, lower, lower went Arrow's head until it was on the ground. When the farmer knew his young horse could stretch no further, he gave him the carrot. "Good boy! Now you're putting all that energy to something good. Maybe someday you'll be a trick horse."

As Farmer Buck walked away, he saw his old pal Brandon whinnying and nodding his head because Brandon wanted a carrot, too! Farmer Buck thought for a moment of all the tricks Brandon had performed to make children smile. Brandon could nod "Yes," and shake hands and give big kisses when you asked for them. Brandon liked kissing Lexie, a little girl who would come to the farm to ride. You see, Lexie was blind, and every week she would come for a riding lesson and farmer Buck would put her up on Brandon's back to help strengthen her legs. Lexie had cerebral palsy and could not walk. Farmer Buck would lead Lexie around on the horse's back, hoping that someday she would be able to ride and walk by herself.

Over the next few weeks, Arrow learned more tricks. Griffen had begun to trust people and was soon getting little treats for letting children pet him. One morning, Lexie and her mom drove up to the farm.

"Hi, Lexie," said Farmer Buck. "Have I got a surprise for you." He carried

the young girl over to Arrow's stall. Lexie was busy eating a jelly donut and did not want to talk with her mouth full. "You know how you have been learning to ride?" the farmer asked Lexie. "Well, Arrow is learning some tricks."
"Some tricks!" Lexie said as she swallowed another mouth full of donut and giggled.

Farmer Buck placed Lexie on Arrow's stall window ledge. "I'll be right back," he said. "I'm going to get him some treats. Don't feed him that donut. I don't want him to get a bellyache."

Arrow loved visitors and came over to Lexie and smelled her sneakers. Then he smelled her pants. Then he smelled her donut, and with a big lick he ate the whole thing. 'Oh, no!' the little girl thought. Lexie didn't know it, but Arrow had jelly all over his lips.

"Are you nice?" Lexie asked. "Do you kiss like Brandon?"

Arrow knew the word "Kiss" and had seen Brandon do it many times. Gently he touched her cheek with his large lips, leaving a big blob of jelly on Lexie's face. The little girl laughed. Arrow then licked the rest of the jelly Lexie had on her hands. She giggled some more and asked him for another kiss. The colt kissed her again, smearing more jelly all over her face.

"You're funny!" Lexie exclaimed.

Arrow thought, "Gee, if I do something nice for her, she does something nice for me." When Farmer Buck returned, he found jelly all over Arrow and Lexie's faces. "Where is your donut?" he asked.

Lexie put her head down and said, "I ate it."

"H-m-m., then why does Arrow have jelly on his mouth?"
Lexie sat silent for a moment, then said, "I'm sorry, Farmer Buck. I didn't want you to get mad, but he took it from me."

"It's better to tell the truth the first time. Then you won't have to feel bad about lying," Farmer Buck told her kindly.

Lexie smiled and hugged him. Arrow then reached over and pulled a hanky from the pocket of Farmer Buck's pants-another trick he had learned! The man dipped it in Arrow's water bucket and wiped their little faces.

Over the next few weeks, Arrow learned more tricks while Lexie was getting better with her riding. One trick Arrow learned was to lie down. Even though it was hard, Farmer Buck wanted to teach him this trick so that the children could see Arrow's famous marking. You see, the colt was getting bigger and some of the kids were not tall enough to see his arrow anymore.

One day Farmer Buck carried Lexie to Arrow's stall and placed her on a bale of hay. He called Arrow over and asked the colt to lie down. Farmer Buck soon noticed that Arrow didn't seem to be listening. Maybe his horse was a little tired and did not want to do his trick. Just then the farmer had to leave the barn for a minute to talk to someone on the phone.
Lexie had some carrots in her pocket. "Hi, Arrow!" she said. "Can I have a kiss today?"

 Arrow kissed her. He liked making Lexie happy and hearing her giggle.
Then Lexie asked Arrow to lie down. She heard a big THUD! Because

Lexie could not see, she reached down to feel the ground. Her hands first discovered Arrow's foot, then his tail, and then his nose. Arrow was lying down! She crawled over, gave him a carrot, and hugged him. He loved getting a hug from Lexie.

When the little horse heard Farmer Buck coming, he slowly stood up. Lexie crawled back to the hay bale and sat down just as the stall door opened. "Okay, Lexie. Time for your lesson. Maybe Arrow will do his trick for you next week."

Lexie smiled. Arrow smiled, too, because he knew his new trick had made someone happy.

Arrow Learns Some Tricks

1. Why do you think it made Arrow so happy to make Lexie happy?

2. Why do you think Arrow would lie down for Lexie but not farmer Buck?

3. What can you do to make someone happy?

60

Lexie and Arrow's Big Day

One day Arrow felt lonely. Everyone was getting ready for the big horse show on Saturday. Everyone that is-but him. Lots of work needed to get done. The horses had to be bathed, the farm had to be extra clean for the people who were coming to see the kids ride. Many of the children were busy practicing. Farmer Buck was working hard painting fences; he didn't even have time for Lexie's riding lesson. She felt sad, but was glad that Farmer Buck invited her to the big event. Although Lexie couldn't see the show, she would enjoy talking to the other children as they rode by. Everyone loved the little girl because she was always happy to hear new sounds and do new things.

Well, the big day was here and the farm was busy. Arrow watched from his stall as many of the horses were groomed: each hair had to be in place, tails needed to be tangle free, saddles were polished and placed on the horses' backs. One by one horses were mounted and headed up the hill to the arena. Kids came with their friends, parents took pictures, but Arrow just watched from his stall and wished that he could go to the show, too.

Soon the horse started to bang on his stall with his hoofs. 'Isn't someone going to pet me?' he wondered. Everyone seemed to be in such a hurry. 'If someone would just say hello to me, that would make me feel happy.' Arrow was only a year old and wasn't trained to carry a rider. His little legs could not hold the weight of a person and a saddle. He could only wish for the day when he would be able to perform with his friends. 'At least I would feel like a part of all the excitement,' he thought.

Just then his pal Jack showed up and jumped up on his stall window. "Hi, Arrow! Are you going to the show?"

"No," Arrow replied sadly. "Farmer Buck is too busy. I don't even think he'll teach me any tricks today." Arrow had learned many tricks-he could shake his head "Yes" and "No," shake hands, bow, lie down, roll over, smile, and even play fetch with a ball.

Arrow heard an announcer's voice come over the loud speaker: "The show is about to start. Please take your seats." Music was playing, and Arrow knew the song. It was the music they play when the children riding on horses carry in the American flags. Arrow often watched the kids practice and dreamed of the day when he could carry a rider holding a flag.

As the show got under way, the little horse couldn't see anything from his stall, although he could hear some things. "At noon today we are going to have a special talent show," boomed the loud speaker. "Make sure you don't miss it!" 'The talent show! Gee, would I like to see that!' Arrow thought. At that moment the young horse heard a giggle, then a small voice call his name. "Arrow, are you here? Arrow, it's me, Lexie."

'Wow,' Arrow thought, 'it's someone for me!' Arrow whinnied loudly and Lexie's mom carried her daughter to his stall .

"Here's Arrow, "she said.

Lexie asked if she could sit with Arrow and feed him carrots and her mom said it was all right. "Just for a little while. I'm going to watch the show, and I'll be back after I say "Hi" to Farmer Buck."

Arrow gave Lexie a big kiss, and she reached in her pocket and fed him a carrot. "I wish I could ride in the show," Lexie told Arrow, "but I can't see where I'm going, and my legs are still weak, so I can't even get up on a horse."

Just then Jack had an idea. "Hey, Arrow!" he said. "Why don't you lie down and let Lexie climb on your back? You could make believe you're in the show and ride her around in your stall."

Arrow and Lexie thought that was a grand idea. Arrow finished up a tasty carrot and Lexie asked him to lie down. THUD! Lexie crawled over to him and climbed on his back. "Okay, Arrow, I'm ready!" Lexie giggled.

Arrow stood up carefully. Lexie gripped his mane with one hand and a carrot with the other. She thought this was fun. The little girl was light and her weight was easy for Arrow to carry.

"We are about to start the talent show. All entries come to the show arena," cried the announcer.

Arrow knew all the names that were called. Taylor, in a costume made by her mother, rode Blueberry. Mae rode her pony Reach for the Stars, and entered with five cats following her; Katie entered on Houdini, who would show everyone how high she could jump; Jen rode in on Boots, who could lick the girl's face like a dog; Dylan came in on Reno, who would race around the barrels; and Matt rode in on Brandon, who would show how fast they could ride.

Goman and Panda carried their riders, two sisters who had two spotted horses; Claire entered in on Darwin, with her guinea pigs Peanut and Chocolate scurrying close behind her; Joe rode in on Jaguar who could trot perfectly ,and Griffen came in with Amy on his back, a little girl he had learned to trust.

'If only the people could see us,' Lexie and Arrow thought. Just then Jack had another idea. He jumped up, slid open the latch to Arrow's stall, and out they went. Arrow pranced by the chickens, the ducks at the pond, and Oscar the barn cat. Lexie held a carrot in her hand like a flag as they trotted up the hill.

Miss Emmy, who ran the tack store, opened her mouth but was so surprised nothing came out. Arrow just trotted past-through the parking lot and around all the horse trailers and people until he approached the arena. When he saw all his friends, he let out a big whinny and trotted in the show ring right up next to them. Everyone gasped as they saw this little horse with no saddle or bridle carrying a small smiling girl holding a carrot high in the air. As all the talent riders began to line up in front of the judge, Arrow continued to trot around to say hello to his friends. The crowd watched with amazement. Lexie's mother could not believe her eyes and neither could the judge. Suddenly, Arrow heard a familiar sound: it was the sound of him getting into trouble.

"ARROW!" yelled Farmer Buck.

The colt stopped in his tracks. In fact, he stopped so fast that Lexie leaned forward and dropped her carrot. Arrow saw the carrot fall under his belly. Although he wanted to eat it very much, he knew he better not move a step.

Then Arrow remembered his trick! Down, down, down he went to get the carrot. When the crowd saw the little colt bow, they cheered with excitement. The judge walked over to Arrow and Lexie and presented them with the First Place Blue Ribbon. They had won the talent show just for being themselves!

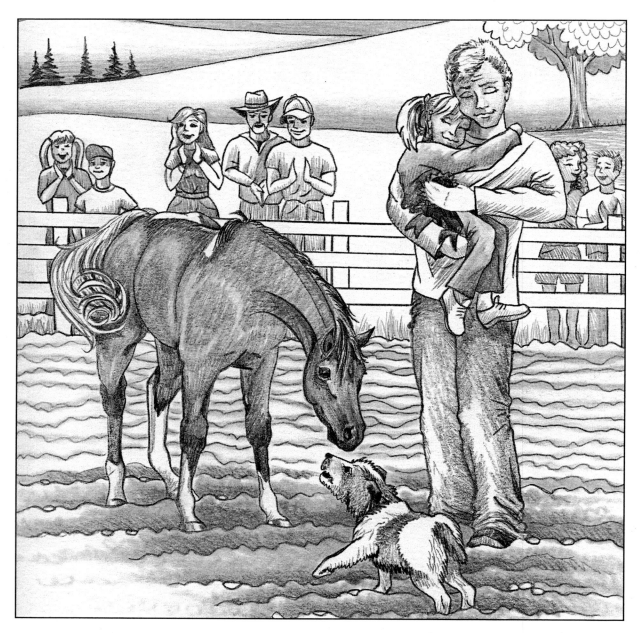

74

Now Farmer Buck approached them. Arrow knew he had done it again, but before the man could say a word, he stretched out his little neck and kissed him. The crowd cheered again. Farmer Buck just shook his head, smiled, and hugged Lexie. Jack ran around and barked with joy because his friends had a day they would never forget and a memory that would last forever.

Lexie and Arrow's big day

1. Why was farmer Buck so upset when he saw Lexie riding on Arrow?

2. Who also was to blame for Arrow and Lexie coming out of the stall?

3. What did it mean when the story said "they had won the talent show just for being themselves"?